My Breakfast

By Anne Giulieri

Look at my breakfast.

Here is my toast.

The toast is hot.

I like my toast with jam on top.

Here is my milk.

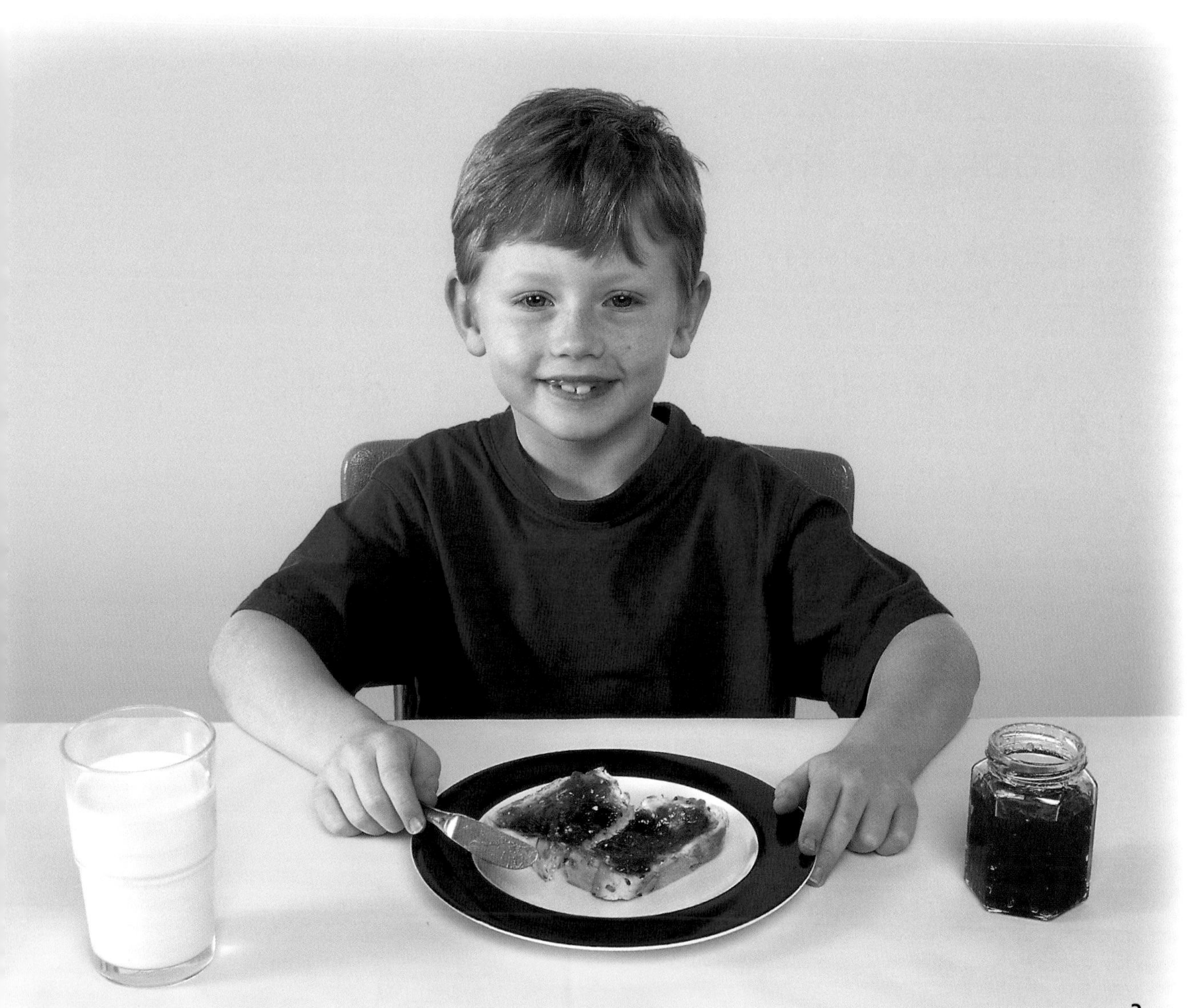

Look at my plate.

Look at my glass.

Where did my breakfast go?

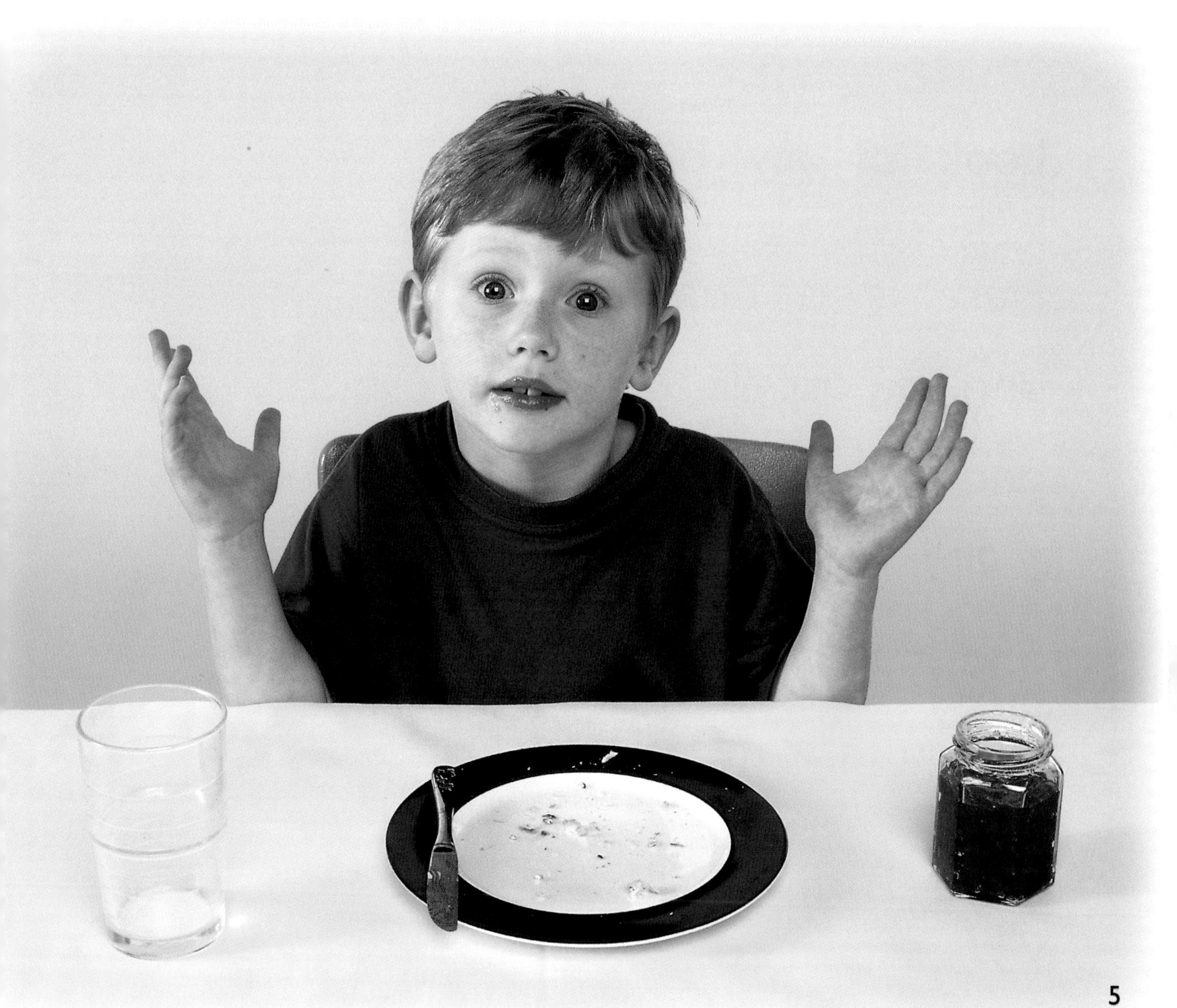

Look at my breakfast.

Here is a banana
and an apple
and an orange.

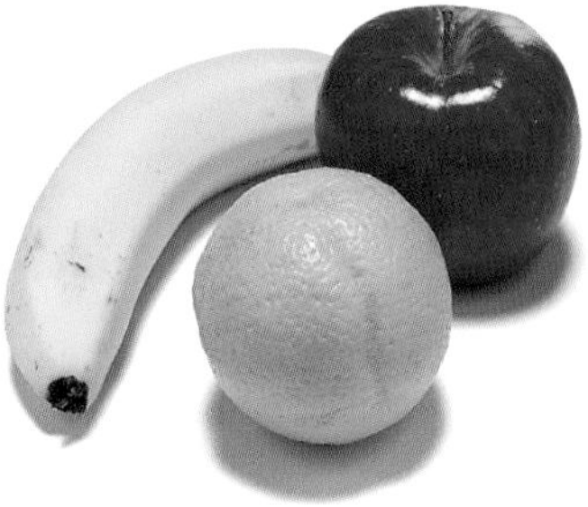

I like my banana
and my apple and my orange
cut into little pieces.

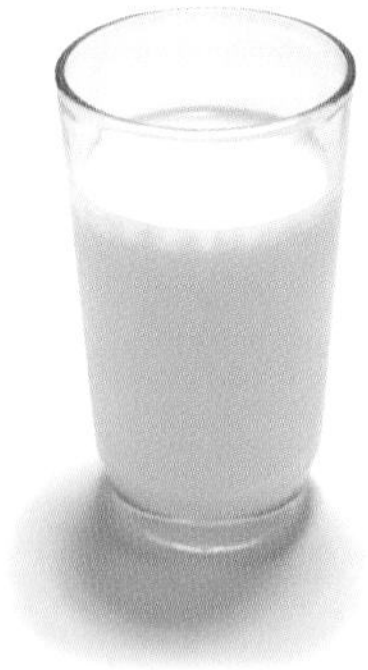

Here is my milk.

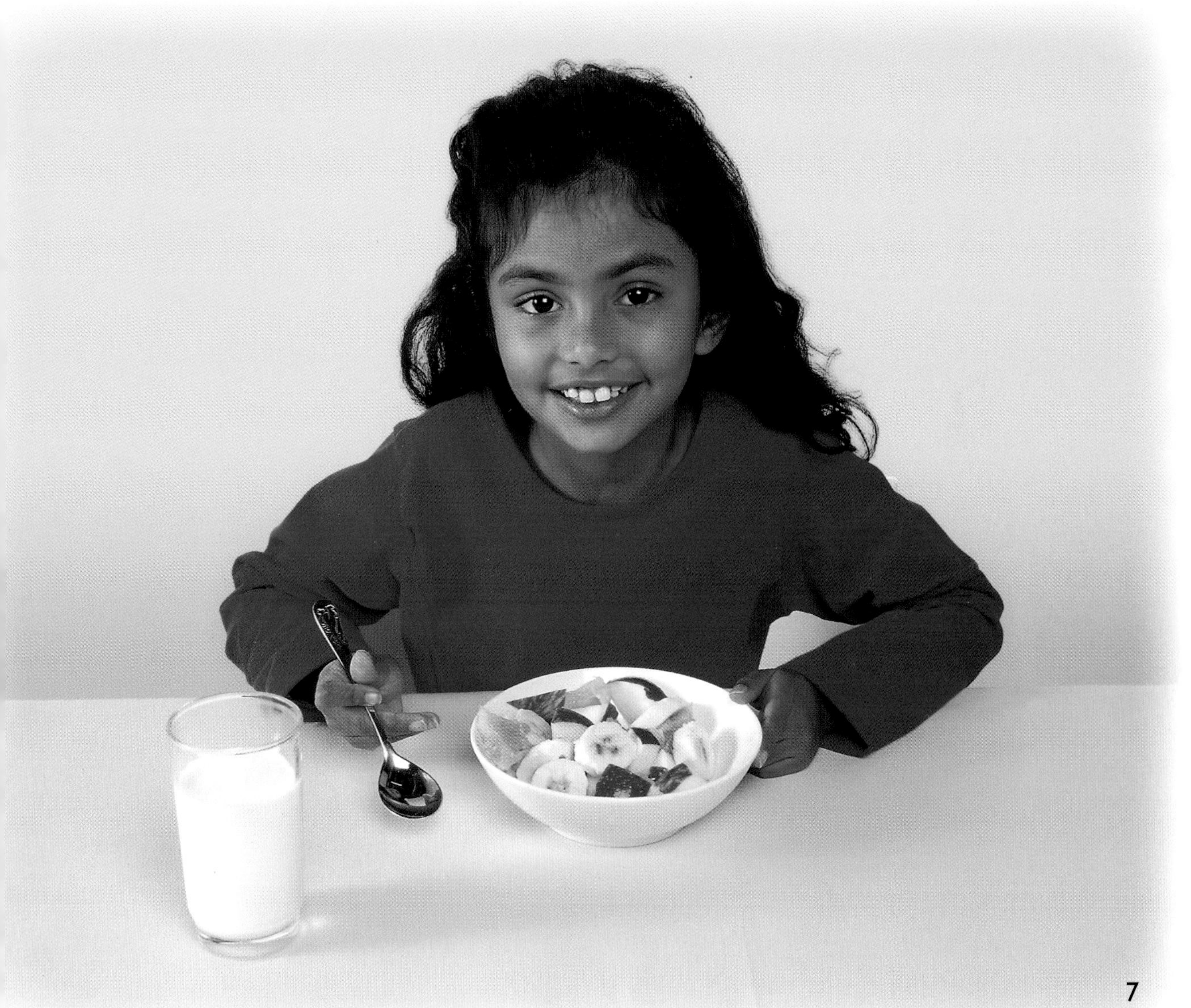

Look at my bowl.

Look at my glass.

Where did my breakfast go?

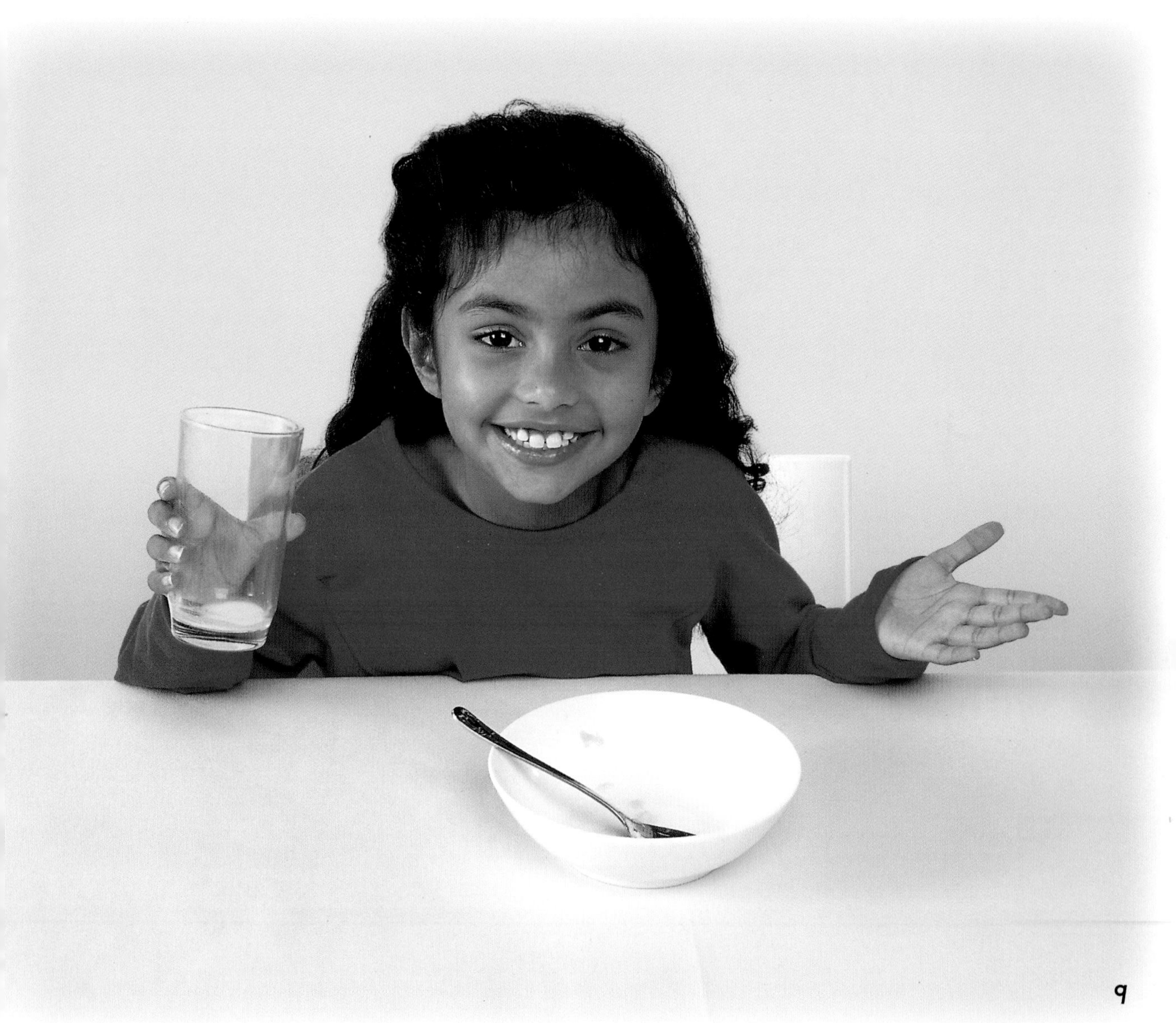

Look at my breakfast.

Here is my toast.

Here is my egg.

My egg is hard-boiled.

I like eating toast
with my egg.

Here is my orange juice.

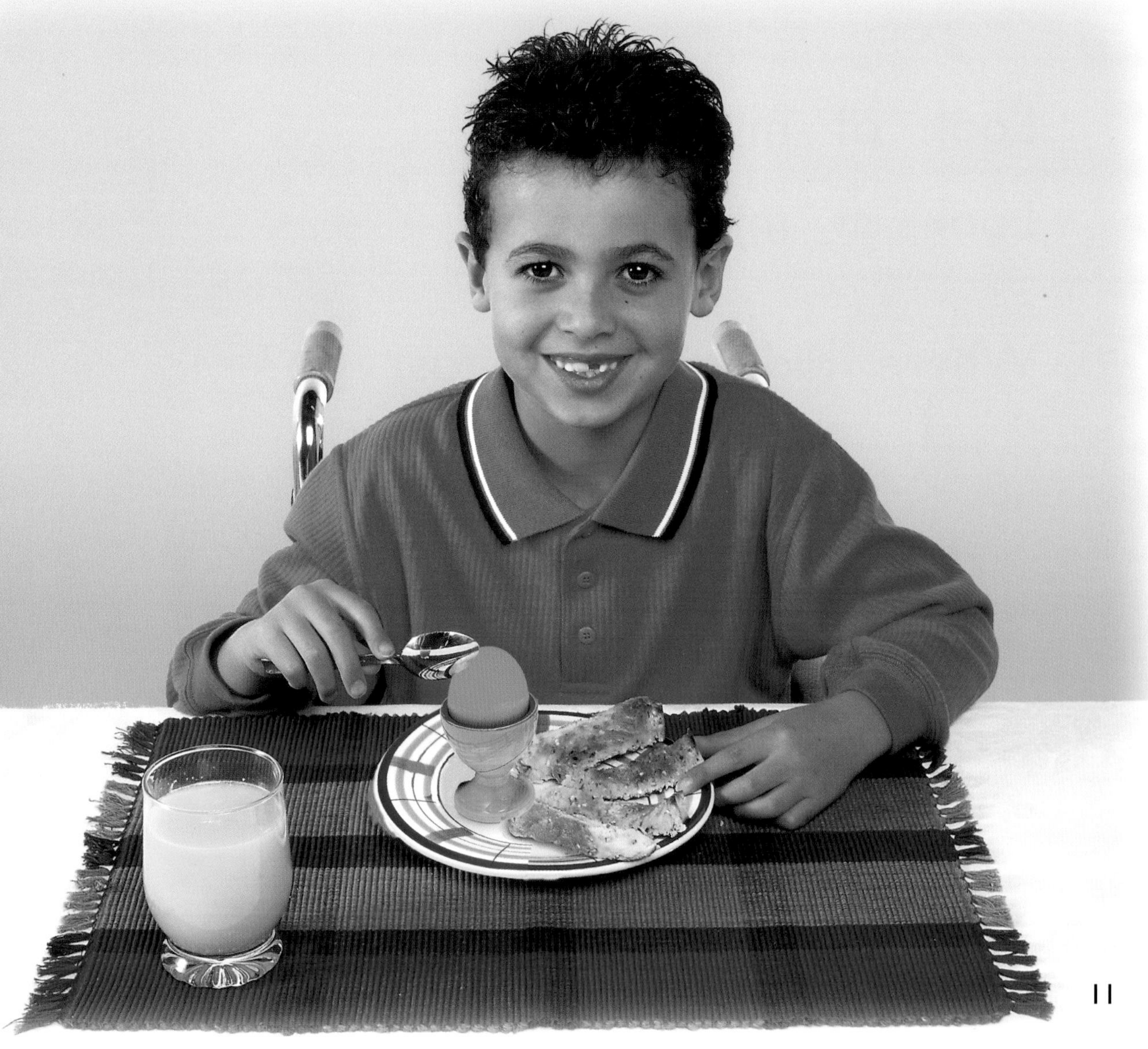

Look at my plate.

Look at my glass.

Where did my breakfast go?

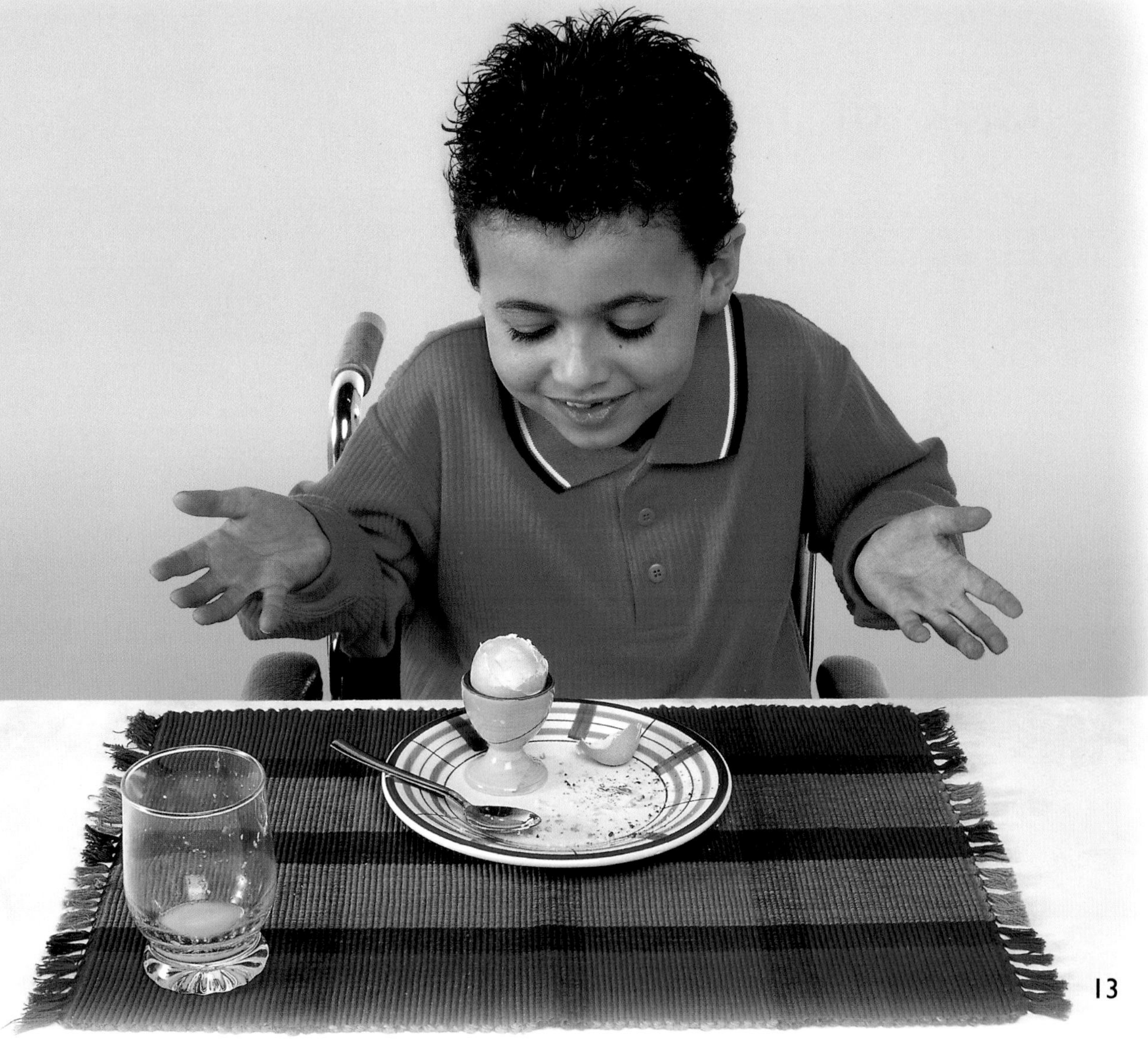

Look at my breakfast.

Here is my big bowl
of oatmeal.

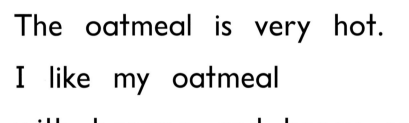

The oatmeal is very hot.
I like my oatmeal
with banana and honey on top.

Here is my orange juice.

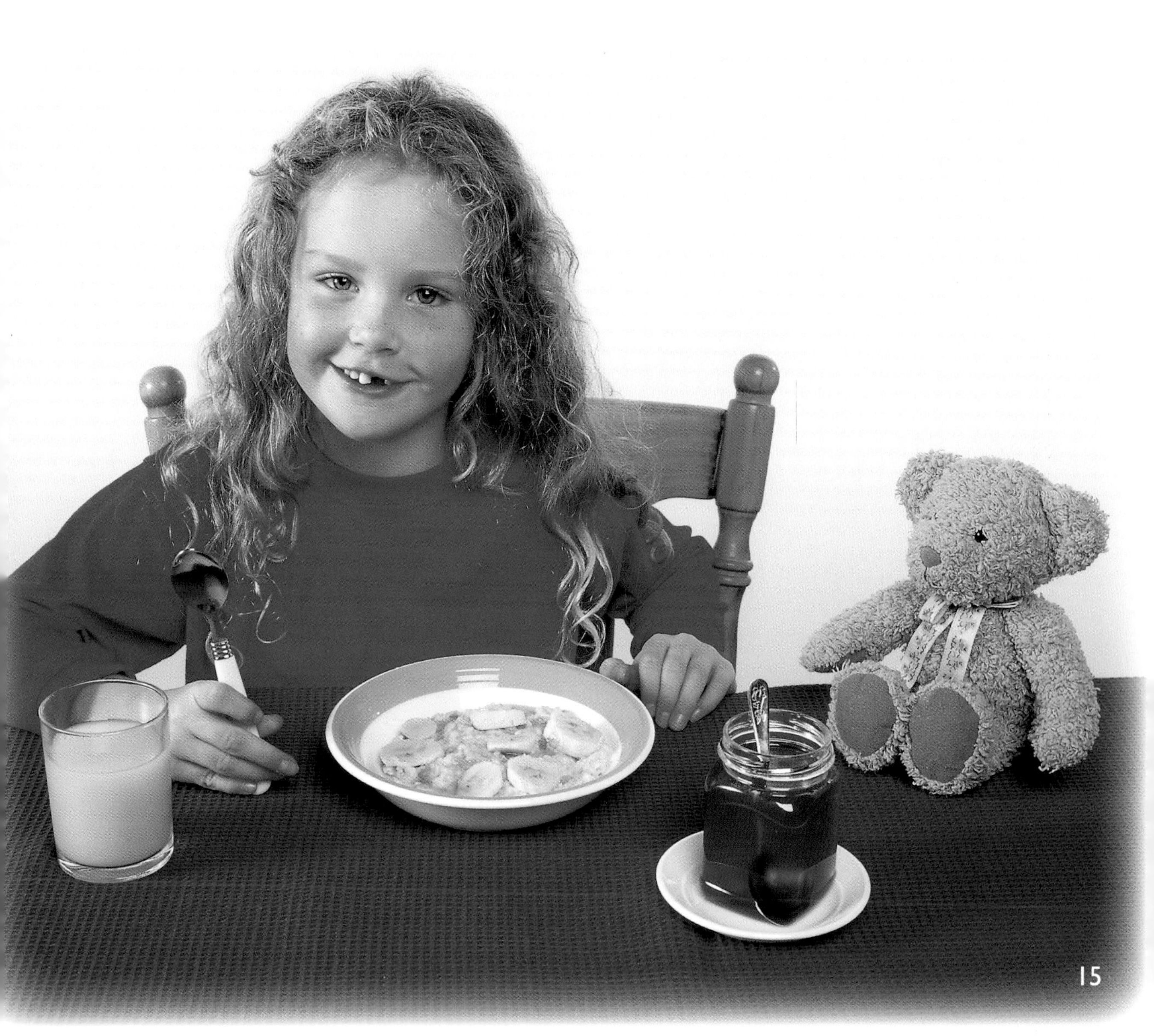

Look at my bowl.
Look at my glass.

Where did
my breakfast go?

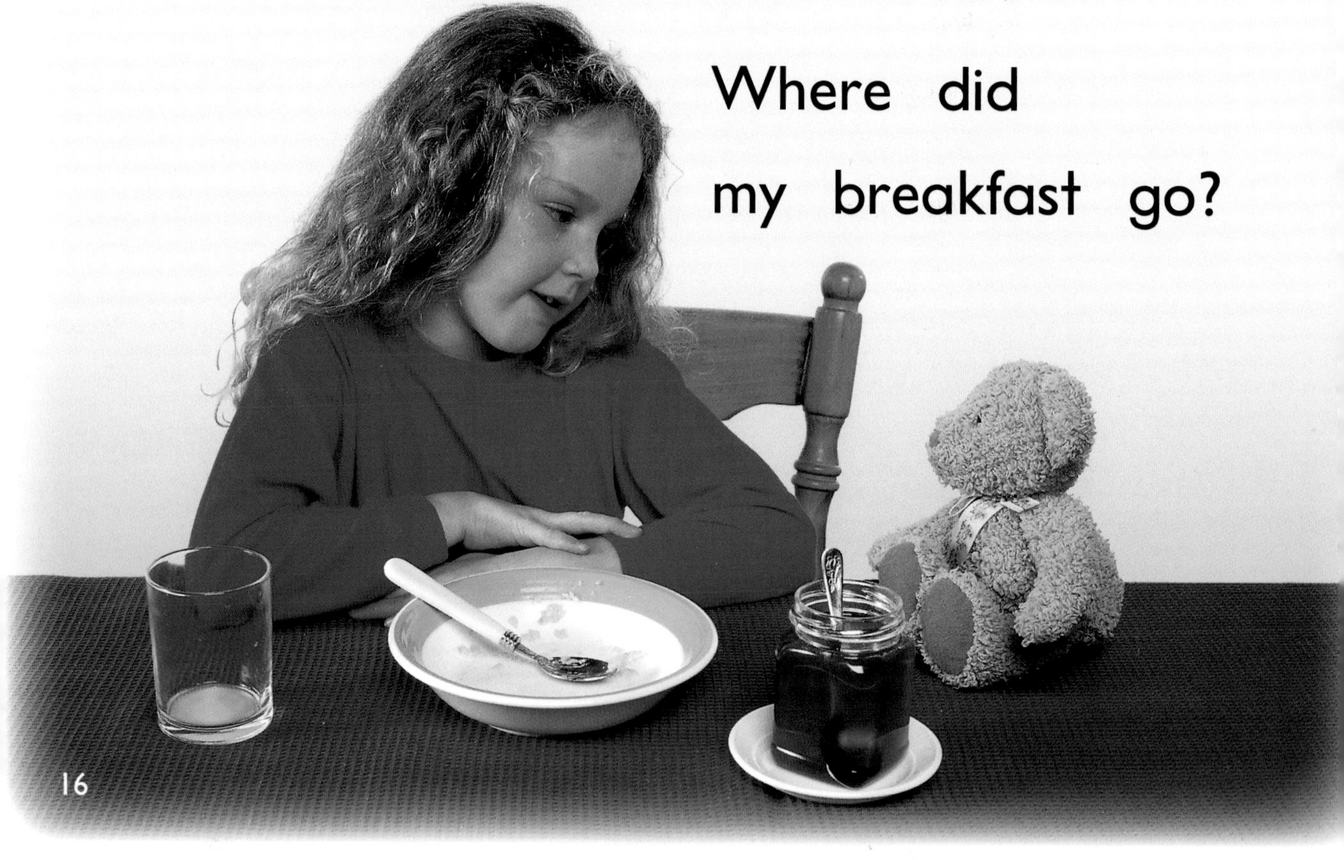